GRACIE
GRUMPOSAURUS

First published in 2013 by Wayland

Text copyright © Brian Moses
Illustrations copyright © Mike Gordon

Wayland
338 Euston Road
London NW1 3BH

Wayland Australia
Level 17/207 Kent Street
Sydney, NSW 2000

Senior editor: Victoria Brooker
Creative design: Basement68
Digital colour: Molly Hahn

British Library Cataloguing
in Publication Data:

Moses, Brian, 1950-
   Gracie Grumposaurus. --
   (Dinosaurs have feelings, too)
   1. Children's stories--Pictorial
   works.
   I. Title II. Series III. Gordon, Mike,
   1948 Mar. 16-
   823.9'2-dc23
ISBN: 978 0 7502 7114 1

Printed in China

Wayland is a division of
Hachette Children's Books,
an Hachette UK company.
www.hachette.co.uk

GRACIE GRUMPOSAURUS

Written by
Brian Moses

Illustrated by
Mike Gordon

WAYLAND

Gracie Grumposaurus was always grumpy.

First thing in the morning
till last thing at night,
Gracie was a grump.

"I don't want to get up," she grumped,
when her mum pulled off her dino-duvet.

"I don't want a pteradactyl's egg," she grumped, after her mum had cooked it just the way she liked it - not too runny and not too soft.

"I'm fed up with all my toys," she grumped,
spinning round and round and knocking
them over with her stubby tail.

When her mother took her to the Dinostore,
everyone would stop them and say,
"How's Gracie today?"

And Gracie would pull her best grumposaurus face. "I think she's tired," Gracie's mum always said.

In the Dinostore, Gracie pulled a carton of root juice out of the trolley. "I don't want that," and SPLAT!, it landed on the floor.

Whatever Gracie's mum wanted
to buy, Gracie didn't.

Gracie was grumpy all day long.

"I don't want to play outside," she grumbled.

"I don't want grassy grits for my dinner," Gracie moaned.

"I want to watch 'Nightmare Dinosaur'
on television," Gracie grumped.

"Well, you can't, Gracie. You're not old enough," her dad said.

Gracie was grumpy in her bath, too.
"I don't want that in here," she said,
flinging her toy duck across the room.

23

Then, finally, when Gracie was tucked up in bed in her very best pyjamas, Gracie's mum tried to read her a story called 'Tyrannosaurus Trouble'.

"I don't want that book," she screeched.

"Oh Gracie," said her mum. "Why are you always such a grump-osaurus? Couldn't you just one day be Gracie Grin-osaurus?"

26

And, for the first time
in a very long time,
Gracie Grumposaurus...

...SMILED!

NOTES FOR PARENTS AND TEACHERS

Read the book with children either individually or in groups. Talk to them about what makes them grumpy. Ask how they feel when they are grumpy.

Can they pull a face that shows what they look like when they're feeling grumpy? Suggest that they look in the mirror and then try to draw that grumpy face.

Help children to compose short poems where each verse begins 'When I'm feeling grumpy ......'

> When I'm feeling grumpy I sulk in my room,
> I hide myself away,
> I don't want to talk.

> When I'm feeling grumpy I frown all day,
> I don't want to play,
> I don't want to do anything.

This can lead to a discussion about how children's grumpy moods can affect others. How do their parents react to their grumpiness? How do brothers and sisters react?

How do other people behave when they're grumpy?
Do parents, grandparents or teachers get grumpy at times?

Compile a list of alternative words for grumpy - sulky, crabby, cross, crotchety, irritable, grouchy. Think about the labels that a grumpy child might be given?

(I started calling my older daughter a grump, and then a grumposaurus when she was young! Another child I knew was labelled 'Sir Grumpalot'.)

Talk about ways in which children might be able to overcome their grumpy feelings. Maybe children could list their three favourite things about their day. If this is done at bedtime, the day ends on a positive note. If it has been a bad day, think how a bad day can be made better.

Some parents say that the way to stop a child being grumpy is to go to the park, or do something outdoors, particularly if a child has been sitting in school all day. Other advice is to play music and do silly dancing to get grumpy children laughing.

Explore grumpiness further through the sharing of picture books and poems mentioned in the book list on page 32.

BOOKS TO SHARE

Grumpy Cat by Britta Teckentrup (Boxer Books, 2008)
Grumpy cat likes to be alone until a cuddly kitten
snuggles up to him.

Grumpy Gertie by Sam Lloyd (Anova, 2013)
Gertie is grumpy all the time until she meets a friendly
monkey who shows her how to turn her frown into a smile.

Silly School by Marie-Louise Fitzpatrick (Frances Lincoln, 2008)
Beth doesn't want to go to silly school! She doesn't want
storytime, painting or singing. So what does she want to do?

The Bad-Tempered Ladybird by Eric Carle (Picture Puffin, 1982)
Still a very popular book in which the bad-tempered ladybird
thinks that it is bigger and better than anyone.

Winnie the Pooh by A.A. Milne (Various editions)
In which we meet gloomy Eeyore who also features
in *The House at Pooh Corner*.

Titles in the series:

Anna Angrysaurus
9780750027112

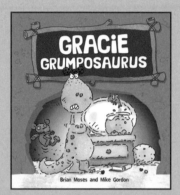

Gracie Grumposaurus
9780750271141

Jamal Jealousaurus
9780750271165

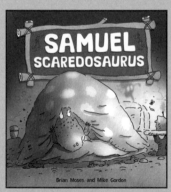

Samuel Scaredosaurus
9780750271134

Sophie Shyosaurus
9780750271172

William Worrydactyl
9780750271158

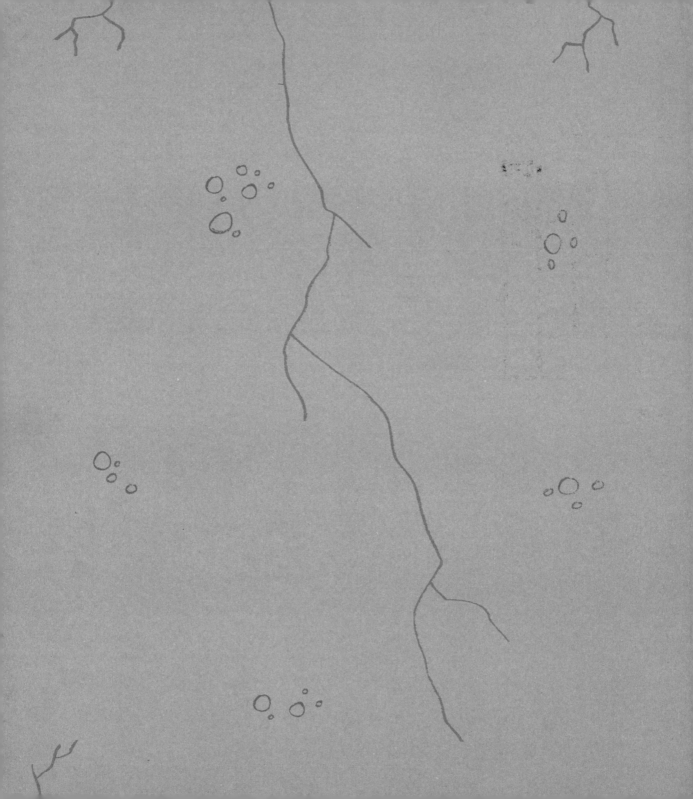